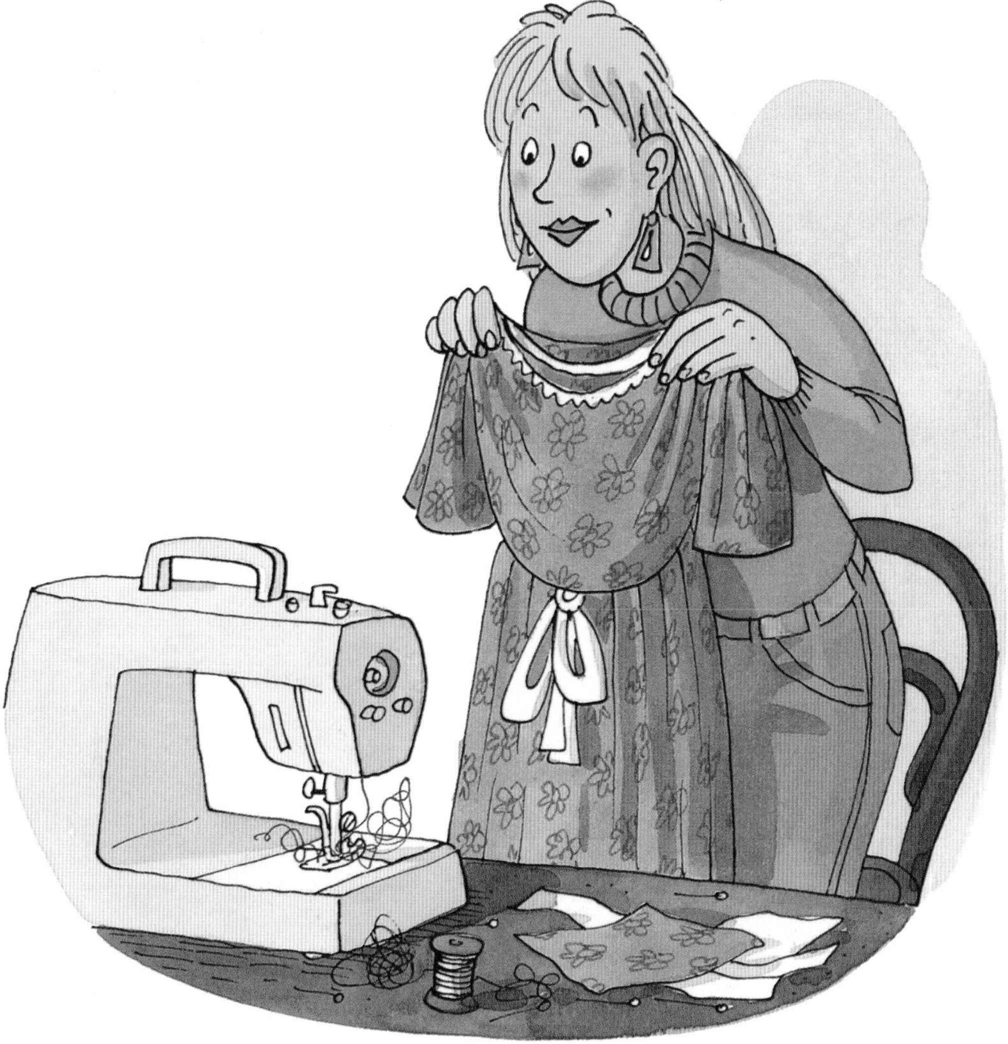

Mum made a dress.

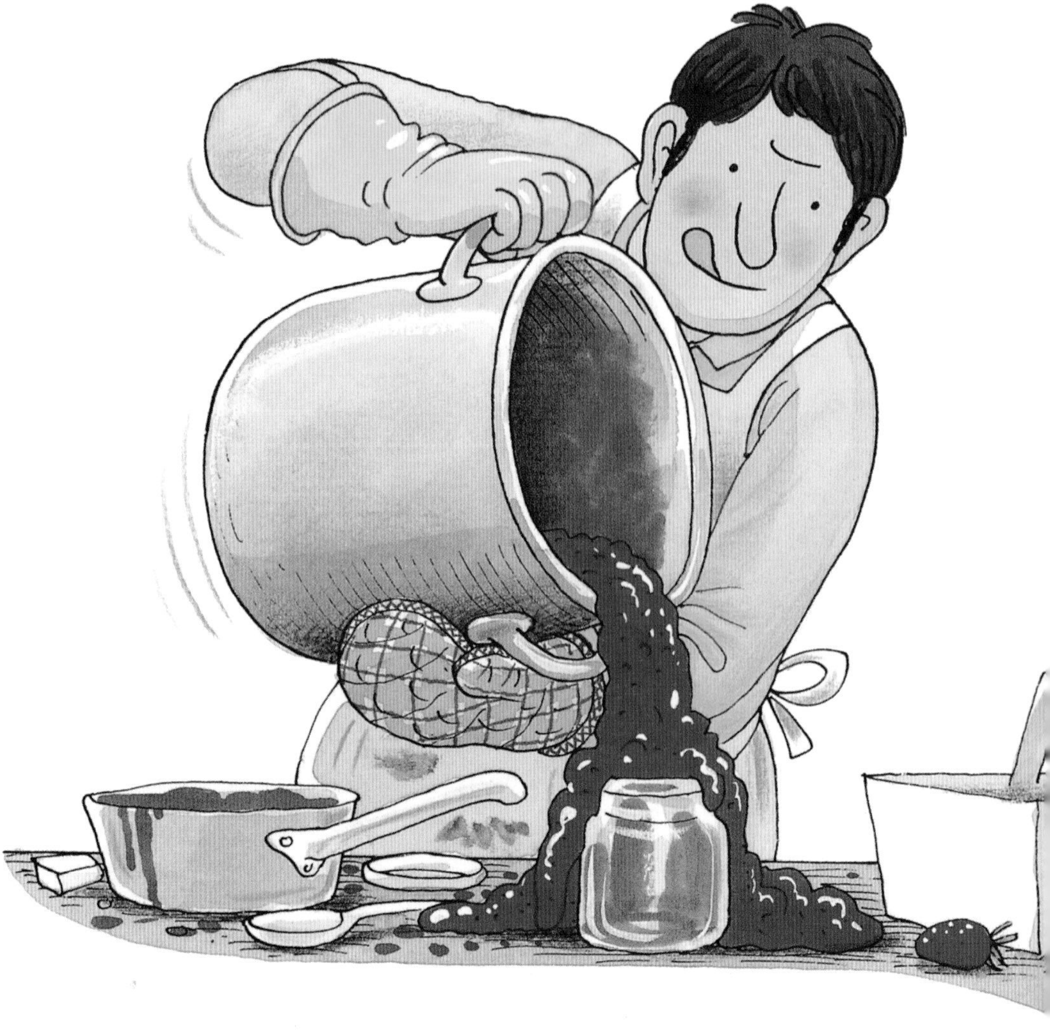

Dad made some jam.

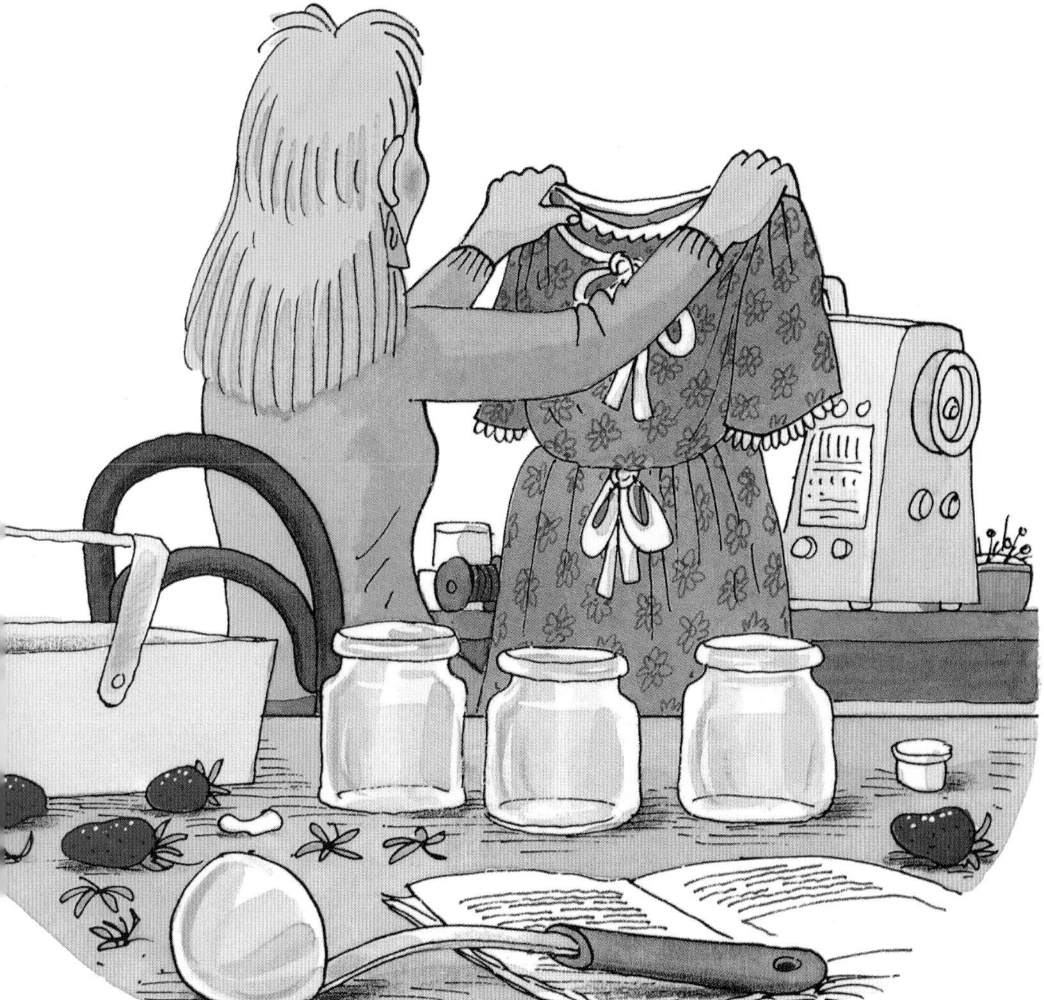

Chip made a scarf.

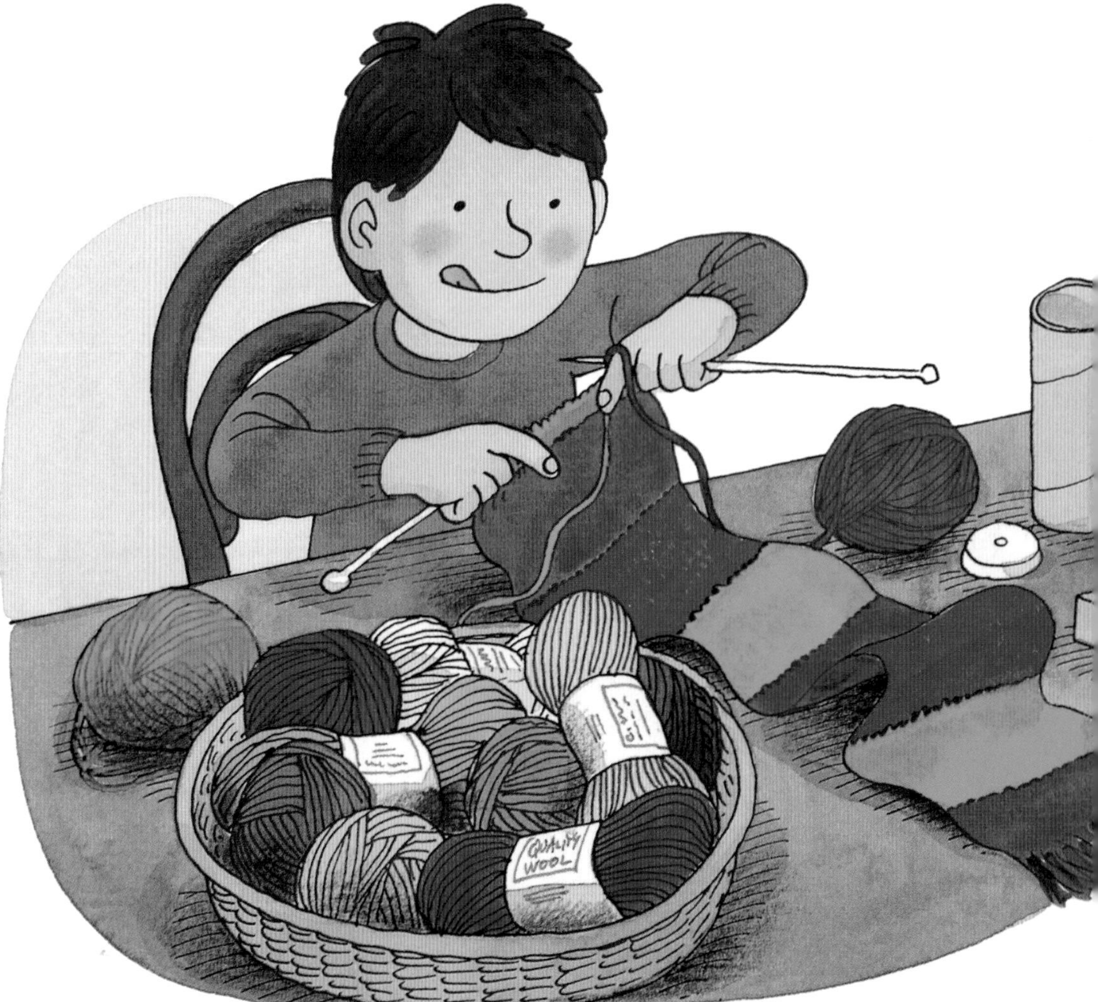

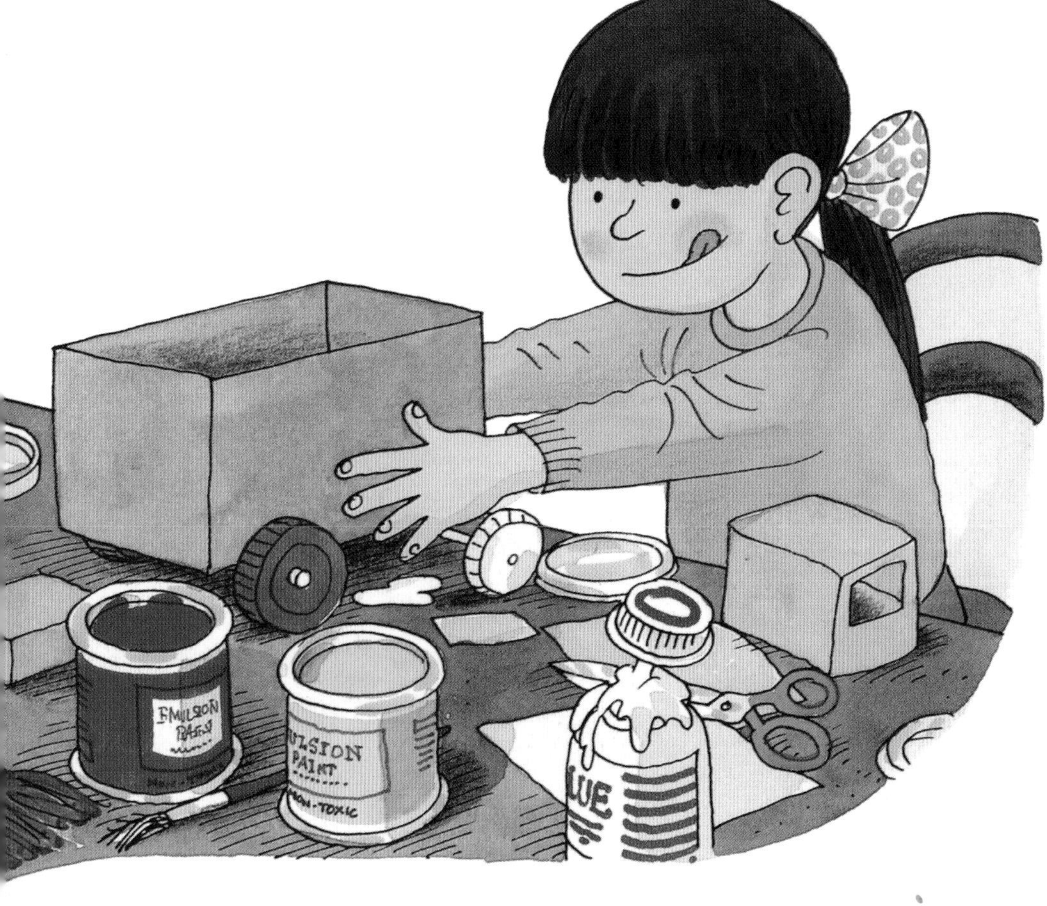

Biff made a lorry.

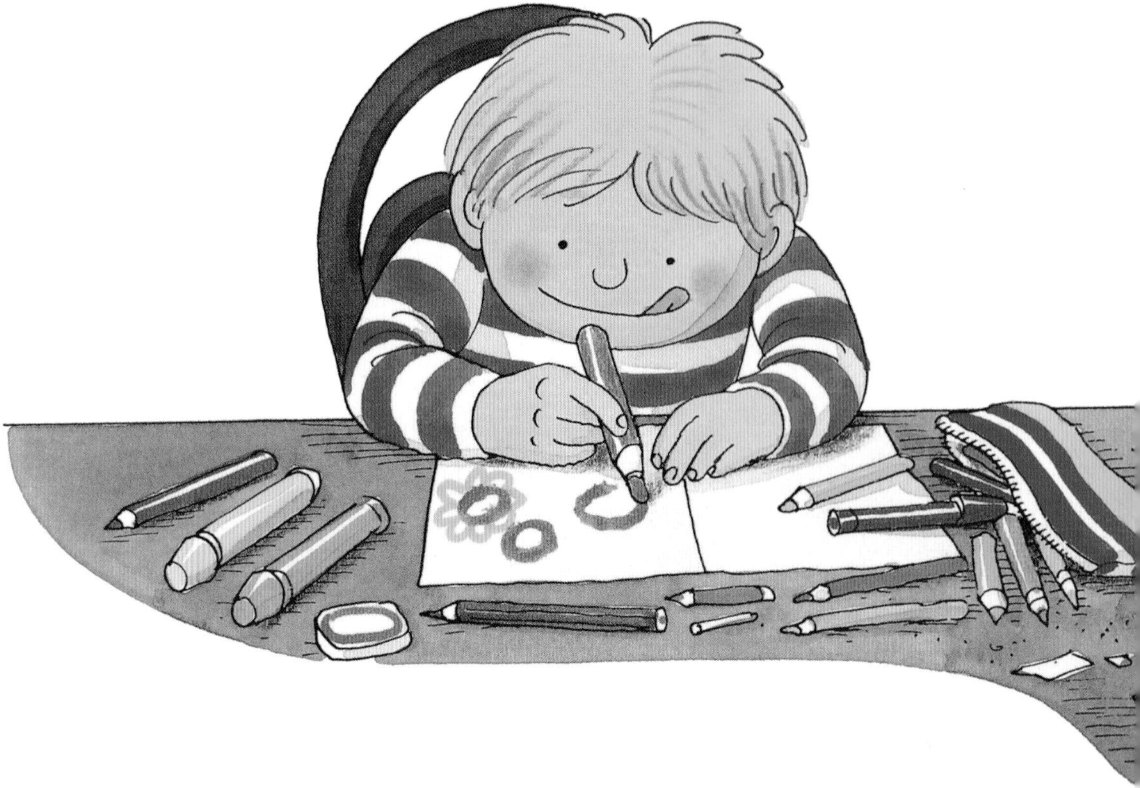

Kipper made a birthday card.

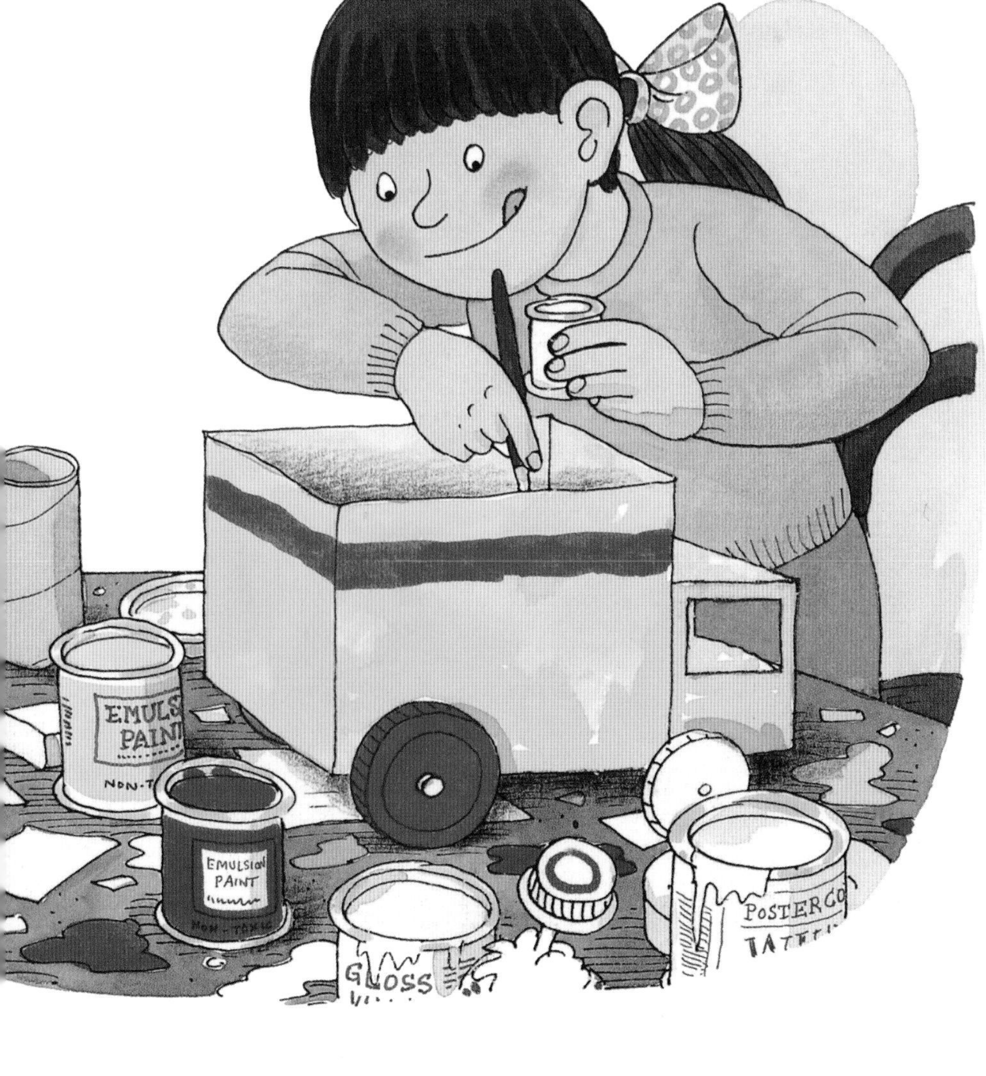
EMULSION
PAINT
GLOSS

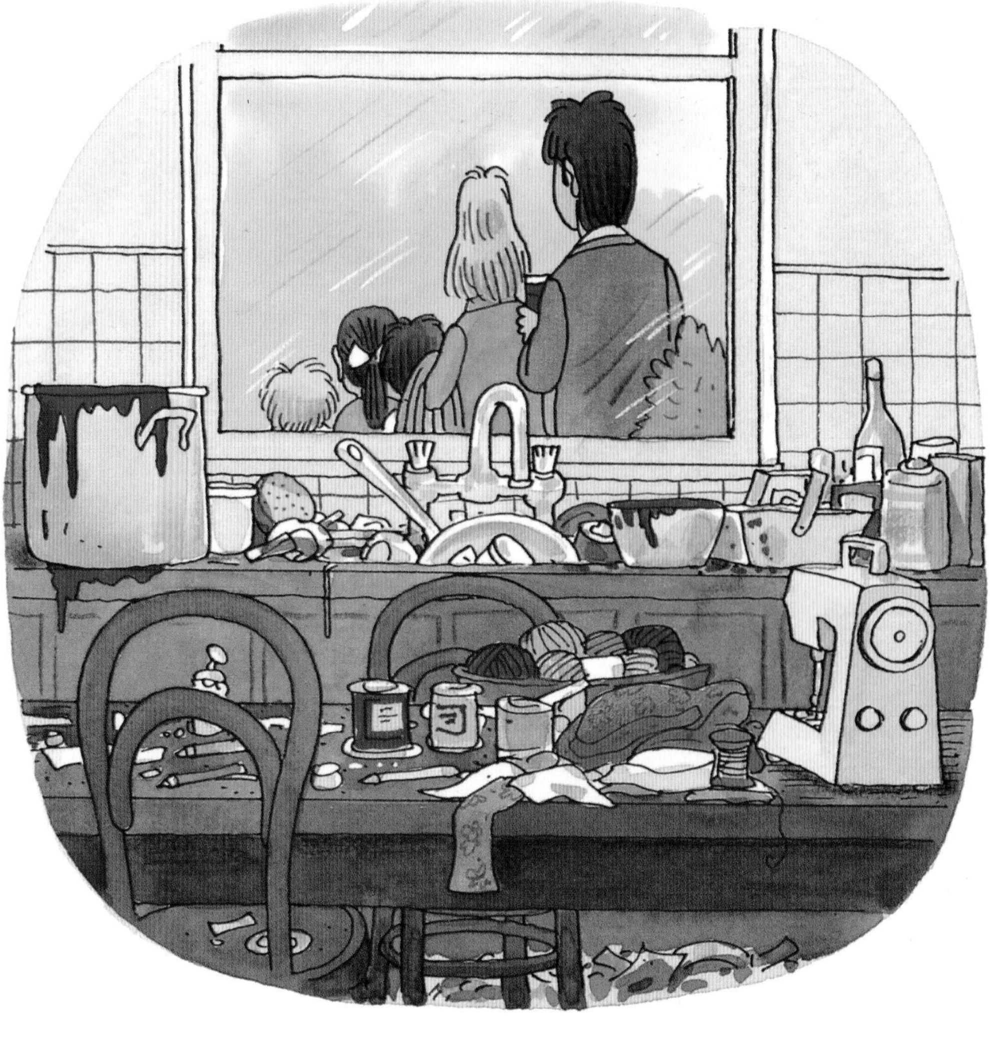

Everyone made a mess.